For my niece, Tamaki—RPW

For my grandmothers, Asako and Kazuko—MS

Text copyright © 2018 by Robert Paul Weston
Illustrations copyright © 2018 by Misa Saburi

Tundra Books, an imprint of Penguin Random House Canada Young Readers,
a Penguin Random House Company

Library and Archives Canada Cataloguing in Publication

Weston, Robert Paul, author
    Sakura's cherry blossoms / Robert Paul Weston ; illustrator, Misa Saburi.

Issued in print and electronic formats.
ISBN 978-1-101-91874-6 (hardcover).—ISBN 978-1-101-91875-3 (EPUB)


    I. Saburi, Misa, illustrator  II. Title.

PS8645.E87S25 2018                jC813'.6                C2017-900555-3
                                                          C2017-900556-1

Published simultaneously in the United States of America by Tundra Books of Northern New York, an imprint of Penguin Random House Canada Young Readers, a Penguin Random House Company

Library of Congress Control Number: 2017931041

Edited by Lynne Missen and Jessica Burgess
Designed by Rachel Cooper
The artwork in this book was rendered in Photoshop.
The text was set in Horley Old Style.

Printed and bound in China

www.penguinrandomhouse.ca

1  2  3  4  5    22  21  20  19  18

 Penguin
Random House
tundra | TUNDRA BOOKS

# Sakura's Cherry Blossoms

Robert Paul Weston
Misa Saburi

tundra

Sakura loved spring,
her favorite time of year.
This made perfect sense.

Her name means cherry blossom,
trees that only bloom in spring.

More than anything
she loved sitting underneath
the tall cherry tree

side by side with Obaachan
whose voice was warm, like sunshine.

Together they sat
in the shade of pink petals
watching them flutter.

They ate bento box lunches.
They told each other stories.

"I've watched this tree grow
all my life," said Obaachan.
"This is how I learned

seeing these blossoms in bloom
is always finest with friends."

Sakura's father
would soon begin a new job
in America.

They would fly across the sea
where a new life awaited.

High up, in the plane
it seemed like a miracle
racing through the clouds

so fluffy and pale, like rice
scooped fresh from Obaachan's pot.

Their new house loomed up
on a street with soaring trees
peppering the ground

with shadows and light, but none
had any cherry blossoms.

Luke, a quiet boy,
lived next door, gazing at night
through a telescope.

Sakura wanted to say
hello, but she was too shy.

Sakura's new school
was a big, boisterous place
where each word was new.

They nipped and snapped on her tongue
like the tang of pickled plums.

*Neko* became "cat."
*Sora* had become "the sky."
*Kutsu* was "a shoe."

Sakura tried very hard
but she often made mistakes.

She missed Obaachan.
She missed the cherry blossoms,
their soft and sweet scent.

She missed stories and picnics
and the whispers of petals.

One day, Luke saw her
sad and still on the front steps.
"When I'm down," he said,

"I find it helps to look up.
If you want, I could show you."

Sakura saw stars,
sprinkles of light, and the moon
pearl-gray and shining.

Its craters were like wide eyes
watching the whole world at once.

"There's a chance," said Luke,
"one of those stars has gone dark
but we still see it

because its last rays of light
have not yet reached us on Earth."

"Flowers are like stars,"
said Sakura. "They blossom,
they sparkle, and then

they fade, so we treasure them
because one day they vanish."

Luke stood very still.
He had never thought of this.
"I suppose," he said,

"When you look up all the time
there are many things you miss."

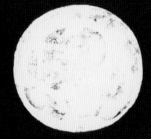

Sakura and Luke.
Soon they were friends who played, laughed
and went exploring.

Sakura, for the first time
had begun to feel at home.

Between friends she found
her words were limber and quick
with no taste at all.

They flipped and curled from her mouth
as effortlessly as breath.

When the winter came
Sakura's mother told her
"We have to go back.

Not for long, but we must go.
Obaachan is very ill."

Sakura's hometown
seemed much smaller than before.
In the cold, bright sun

even the tall cherry tree
was shivering and leafless.

Mother had been right.
Obaachan was very sick,
dozing in her bed.

But hearing Sakura's voice
she awoke, her eyes dancing.

"My little blossom!"
she cried. "Seeing you again
makes me so happy.

It is all that I wanted.
Only this, and nothing more."

This time, on the plane
Sakura did not marvel
at the cotton clouds.

She slept, dreaming of a sky
churning with every season.

Luke was excited
seeing Sakura again
but when he asked her

to go exploring with him
she said no, she was too sad.

She was worried too.
Might she forget Obaachan?
Her face? Her laughter?

With no cherry trees nearby
what was there to remind her?

"Don't worry," said Luke.
"I have a surprise for you.
Just wait until spring."

Sakura did. She waited.
The days grew warmer, and then . . .

The entire city
burst to life, flowers blooming
on every corner.

By the river, both its shores
blazed bright with cherry blossoms!

Huge crowds of people
had gathered to admire them.
There were pink balloons,

music, picnics, a parade
and even a marching band!

Sakura and Luke
found a quiet place to sit
with their families.

They ate lunch and told stories.
They chatted, they played, they laughed.

And Sakura knew
what Obaachan said was true.
On a warm spring day

watching cherry blossoms bloom
is always finest with friends.

## Tanka

This story was written in a series of tanka poems. A tanka is a traditional Japanese poem with five lines and thirty-one syllables. The first three lines follow the same pattern as a haiku (5-7-5), but a tanka has two additional lines, each with seven syllables, for example,

*I am a tanka*
*a poem with five short lines*
*count my syllables*

*you will know I am finished*
*when you get to thirty-one*

The first tanka poems were composed in the seventh century, more than 1,300 years ago! If you enjoyed Sakura's story, perhaps you could compose some tanka of your own.